'The author is a comparative newcomer ~~to~~ this evider[...]'

'A handsome creation.'

The Children's Bookseller

'Perfect for newly developing readers and great to share.'

Primary Times

'Watch out for this new kid on the children's books block, you will be won over!'

Librarymice.com

'I loved everything about this book.'

Bookbag

*For Nanna Betty
and her handbag full of
dog biscuits.*

HODDER CHILDREN'S BOOKS

First published in Great Britain in 2012 by Hodder Children's Books
This edition published in 2015 by Hodder and Stoughton

13

Text and illustrations copyright © Alex T. Smith, 2012

The moral rights of the author have been asserted.

A CIP catalogue record for this book
is available from the British Library.

ISBN 978 0 340 99903 5

Printed in China

MIX
Paper from
responsible sources
FSC® C104740

Hodder Children's Books
An imprint of
Hachette Children's Group
Part of Hodder & Stoughton
Carmelite House
50 Victoria Embankment
London EC4Y 0DZ
An Hachette UK Company
www.hachette.co.uk

# CLAUDE.

## at the Circus

ALEX T. SMITH

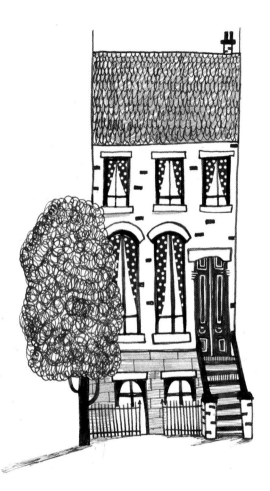

In a house on Waggy Avenue,
number 112, there lives a dog.

A small dog.

A small, plump dog.

A small, plump dog who wears a beret and a rather fetching sweater.

His name is Claude, and here he is.

beret →

rather fetching
sweater

Claude's best friend is Sir
Bobblysock. He is both a sock
and quite bobbly.

*Sir Bobblysock*

Claude and Sir Bobblysock don't
live in their big house all by
themselves; Mr and Mrs Shinyshoes
live there too.

Usually, Mr and Mrs Shinyshoes get up bright and early, leap into their smartest clothes and shiniest shoes and hotfoot it out of the door to work. Sometimes though, mainly on nice sunny Saturdays, Mr and Mrs Shinyshoes pop on their comfy clothes and pack a picnic.

'Let's go on a day trip!'
Mr Shinyshoes says.
'Lovely idea!' says Mrs Shinyshoes.
'Shall we take Claude?'

'No,' whispers Mr Shinyshoes.
'Let's leave him here to sleep.
You know how awfully tired he gets.
We won't be long.'

And so Mr and Mrs Shinyshoes
tiptoe out of the house,
hop in the car and pootle off
to the countryside for the day.

But Claude hasn't really been
asleep. He's been listening with
his floppy ears and peeping
with his beady eyes.

As soon as the front door closes,
Claude jumps out of bed, puts on
his beret, and decides what
adventure he shall have.

One bright Saturday morning when Mr and Mrs Shinyshoes were off in the country, Claude popped on his beret and  thought about what he wanted to do. He felt like he needed a treat as he had been very busy the day before, giving his bed a good spring clean.

He had plumped up the pillow,
shaken the blanket and tidied
up his top-secret hidy-hole.

Out went several packets of half-
chewed biscuits and a juicy bone
baguette which was rather past
its best.

Sir Bobblysock had sat in a comfy
armchair and told him what to do.
He would have loved to help, but
he didn't want to get in the way.

'I think I will go to the park today,'
Claude said.

So off he went.

Sir Bobblysock came along too,
although he was worried that all the
flowers might set off his hayfever
and make him sneeze.

LOVELY PARK

AMAZING ALAN'S
AMAZING
CIRCUS

HERE
TODAY!

15

Claude had never been to the park
before.

He was surprised by how much like
a big garden it was. There was grass
absolutely everywhere and several
trees, too.

And as it was such a sunny day, the whole place was full of people enjoying themselves.

Claude was pleased to see there was also a van selling ice creams.
His tummy rumbled. Even though it wasn't quite eleven o'clock, he decided it was time for a snack.

But just as he and Sir Bobblysock stepped on to the path, a group of people in very strange clothes ran past them.

Claude had never seen anything like it.

There were even some people running with their babies in buggies!

Before he could say "excuse me" or ask politely what they were doing, he found himself tangled up amongst them.

Soon he and Sir Bobblysock were
jogging along with the group.
Sir Bobblysock had to hop like mad
to keep up.

Round and round the park they
went, running all the time.
Claude quite enjoyed it, but he
did wonder what on earth they
were running for.

Had a lion escaped from the zoo?

Were all these people being chased
by the police?

Maybe everyone had realised they weren't wearing proper clothes and were running home to get changed.

Claude didn't know.

What he did know was that his tummy was still grumbling and now he couldn't even see the ice cream van. There was nothing for it but to escape from all these mad running people.

Quickly, he tucked Sir Bobblysock
under his arm, and was just about
to leap out from the crowd when his
foot got caught in one of the
jogger's dangly shoelaces.

Everyone went flying. Claude and Sir Bobblysock hurtled through the air, bumped down on the grass and tumbled over and over until...

...they landed neatly in a flowerbed!

It was very comfortable there and the flowers smelt lovely.

Claude looked around and decided the flowerbed would be the perfect spot to take a nap. After all that running about, he and Sir Bobblysock were very tired.

Forgetting all about ice cream, Claude settled down and closed his eyes. Sir Bobblysock, who always found sleeping in sunlight difficult, popped on his eye mask and took some deep breaths to relax.

But the nap didn't last very long.

'Ahem! Ahem!' coughed a man in a smart uniform and a peaked cap. It was the park keeper, and he did not look happy.

Claude and Sir Bobblysock  woke up.

Sir Bobblysock was not pleased.
He always liked to nap
for exactly forty-six
minutes, and he had
only managed five.

The park keeper didn't say
anything. He just pointed to a sign
that Claude hadn't seen earlier,
when he had been flying through
the air.

SLIGHTLY IMPOLITE NOTICE

DO **NOT**
SLEEP IN THE
FLOWERBEDS
THANK YOU

Claude sighed and stood up. He dusted down his lovely jumper, straightened his beret and set off along the path, with Sir Bobblysock hopping behind. Their nap would have to wait until later. It was time for ice cream!

Claude spotted the ice cream van in
the distance.
'Come on!' he said to Sir Bobblysock,
and marched towards it.

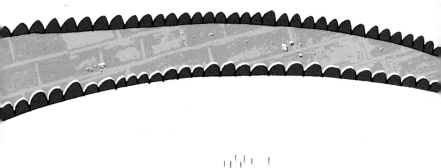

On the way they found themselves striding across a funny sort of field. There were holes everywhere in the grass and somebody had littered the place with balls.

Claude quickly filled up the holes and tidied the balls away under his beret.

Some very rude people didn't seem very happy about what he had done, so Claude and Sir Bobblysock quickly scampered away to the ice cream van.

17TH

37

When they got there, Claude bought himself a soft whippy ice cream with raspberry sauce and a chocolate flake. Sir Bobblysock really wanted a cup of tea but had a sticky, stripy lolly instead.

After they had finished, Claude put Sir Bobblysock's lolly wrapper in the bin.

He also threw away another piece of rubbish he had found stuck to a bench, wanting to be helpful, and not wanting to get told off by the park keeper again.

They were wondering what to do
next, when someone whizzed by on
a scooter. And then someone else
whizzed by.

It looked like fun, so Claude and
Sir Bobblysock watched as the two
children zipped here and there,
doing tricky tricks and daredevil
stunts.

'Would you like a go?' asked the little girl.

Claude nodded politely and climbed on to the scooter. He was a bit wobbly at first but was soon zooming about like nobody's business!

Sir Bobblysock had a turn, but he wasn't keen. He much preferred having a nice sit down and a biscuit.

Claude was just about to hand the
scooter back to the little girl
when he heard a noise from behind
him. It was somebody shouting...

And a baby suddenly zoomed past!
One of the running mummies had
let go of her buggy!

The baby looked very happy,
but he was heading straight for the
duck pond.

'Quick!' shouted the little girl.
'Save him!'

Claude grabbed Sir Bobblysock and
set off.

Sir Bobblysock took control of the handlebars, Claude pushed off with his foot along the path, and within a minute they had caught up with the escaped baby.

Claude reached out and caught the
baby just before he fell in the water.

Everyone clapped and shouted,
'Hooray for Claude and Sir
Bobblysock!'

Only the baby was a bit miffed
because he had been enjoying his
ride.

Claude pulled the balls he had
tidied up earlier out from under his
beret and gave them a quick juggle.
Then Sir Bobblysock did a high-
stepping jig.

Everyone laughed and cheered again, but Claude was beginning to feel rather shy so he and Sir Bobblysock went to find the café for a spot of lunch.

They were sitting outside, munching happily, when a very strange-looking man came and sat at the table next to them.

Claude did his very best not to stare, but of course Sir Bobblysock couldn't help himself. He turned right around in his seat and had a good look over the top of his hot dog. The man at the next table noticed.

'Hello,' he said, holding out his hand. 'I am the Amazing Alan, of Alan's Amazing Circus. May I offer you and your friend two tickets for this afternoon's performance? Ringside seats, on the house!'

Claude was delighted, as he'd never
been to the circus before. He and
Sir Bobblysock decided to go to the
circus tent early, to explore.

They ducked under the striped
canvas.

All the performers were getting
ready for the show in their caravans,
so there was no one about.

Claude couldn't help noticing that
although the tent was very exciting,
it was also very untidy and quite
grubby in places.

There was only one thing for it. He
would have to give the tent a jolly
good spring clean.

Claude fished a feather duster out
from under his beret and dusted the
ring. Then he swept all the sawdust
on the floor into a big pile in the
centre. He climbed a long ladder
and gave the trapeze a good polish,
and the high wire a once over with
a damp cloth.

Behind a curtain, he found a pile of plates covered in fluffy custardy cream. Claude decided the cream smelt a bit funny, so he threw it away and washed up the plates. Soon they were all neatly stacked in a pile, sparkling clean.

By now the rest of the audience had started to come in, so Claude and Sir Bobblysock took their seats. The Amazing Alan waved to them, but he had to hurry off to help the Human Cannonball find her glittery crash helmet.

Clown Noses

Hooter

Claude and Sir Bobblysock watched in amazement as acrobats and gymnasts and dancers and clowns came tumbling into the ring. They were all dressed in wonderful costumes. Sir Bobblysock, who liked sequins and feathers and that sort of thing, was very impressed. The Amazing Alan cracked his whip, and the show began.

But it was a disaster!

The clowns weren't funny at all.
Their custard pies had been washed
up, and when they threw the clean
plates at each other they ended up
with sore noses.

The trapeze artists were no better.
The trapezes were so slippery they
couldn't keep hold of them,
so they landed with a bump in the
sawdust and bruised their bottoms.

The audience began to realise
something was wrong.

The tightrope walker slipped off the damp wire and dangled by her knickers until their elastic snapped. Then she fell on to a trampoline, bounced through the tent roof and landed in the duck pond.

People in the audience began to mutter, and the Amazing Alan was very embarrassed.

'This has never happened before,' he apologized to Claude and Sir Bobblysock. 'I've got no idea what's wrong with my performers today.'

Claude did, and was beginning to feel a bit hot behind the ears.

'Would you take over?'
Alan asked. 'Otherwise, I'm
afraid the audience will ask
for their money back.'

Claude was astonished.
He had never performed
in a circus before.

'Don't worry, you'll be brilliant,'
said Alan. 'I saw you juggling in
the park. Here, wear this hat.
And take the little fellow with you –
he's funny.'

So Claude and Sir Bobblysock
found themselves standing in the
middle of the ring...

At first Claude wasn't sure what to do, so he just smiled politely and wagged his tail.

'Get on with it!' hissed the Amazing Alan, who was watching nervously.

Claude smiled again, then he did some star jumps and some twirling around on the spot.

The audience was impressed.

Then Claude cleverly rubbed some chalk on the bottom of his shoes, so his feet wouldn't slip.

He clambered up the ladder and stepped on to the tightrope.
It was ever so high, so he shut his eyes and pretended he was just tip-toeing down a very thin bit of road.

To his surprise, he found that he was quite good at it. He hung from one paw and stood on one leg (not at the same time).

Then, because he was getting tired,
he sat down halfway along and
drank a cup of tea. The crowd went
wild when he dunked his biscuit.

Next, Claude and Sir Bobblysock did a clown routine. They whizzed around the ring in a car that was too small for them, and fell over a lot.

Then they threw some freshly-made custard pies at each other. The pies were so delicious, Claude couldn't help catching one in his mouth and gobbling it up (plate and all!).

The audience thought this was very funny.

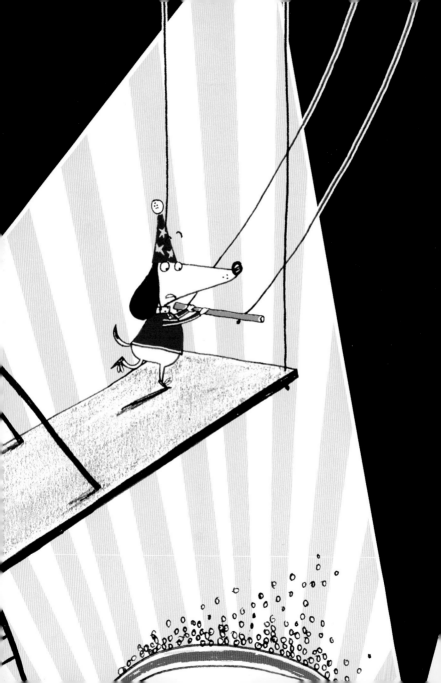

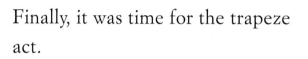

Finally, it was time for the trapeze act.

Bravely, Claude and Sir Bobblysock climbed up the ladders, reached for a trapeze each, took a deep breath and swung out over the audience.

They were marvellous, flying through
the air like a couple of monkeys!

Everyone leapt to their feet and
clapped until their hands were sore.
'Hooray!' they cried. 'Hooray for
Claude and Sir Bobblysock!'

The Amazing Alan was delighted.
'You are both absolute stars!' he
boomed, as Claude and Sir
Bobblysock took a bow.

'Please will you join our circus? You will be very famous if you do!'

Claude thought for a moment. Although circus life sounded fun, he would miss Mr and Mrs Shinyshoes too much if he went away. So he said thank you very much and that he had enjoyed himself a lot, but he would rather just go home. Besides, Sir Bobblysock was in need of one of his long lie-downs.

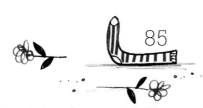

Suddenly Claude gasped. There was a problem! He had forgotten the time.

How could he get home before Mr and Mrs Shinyshoes came back from the country?

Luckily the Human
Cannonball had an idea.

As soon as Claude had said
his goodbyes to all the friendly
circus people, he put on the
Human Cannonball's glittery crash
helmet, tucked Sir Bobblysock safely
up his jumper, and clambered into
the huge cannon.

Claude flew through the air and
landed with a CRASH
in his cosy bed in the kitchen,
just as Mr and Mrs Shinyshoes were
opening the front door.

He quickly pretended to be asleep.

'Um... Mrs Shinyshoes?' said Mr
Shinyshoes, looking at Claude.
'Do you happen to know why
Claude is wearing a glittery crash
helmet?'

'No idea, darling!' said Mrs
Shinyshoes, looking up.
'Do you know why there's a Claude-
shaped hole in the roof?'

Mr Shinyshoes said he didn't have a
clue.

But Claude did, so he gave Sir
Bobblysock a secret wink.

# How to be a Clown

1. Paint your nose red with face paints.

2. Tell some silly jokes.

What kind of dog takes a bubblebath?

A shampoodle!

What swings from a trapeze and miaows?

An acrocat!

Why do dogs wag their tails?

Because no one else will do it for them!

3. Fall over a lot.

## TA-DA! You are now a clown!

Remember to keep your eye out for Claude
and Sir Bobblysock. You never know
where they might pop up next!

# CLAUDE

in the city

Claude is a dog who wears a red beret. He has a friend called Sir Bobblysock who is a sock!

It's a funny book with lots of exciting pictures.

It has two parts and I read it in two nights all by myself.

IT'S BRILLIANT!!

Poppy age 6